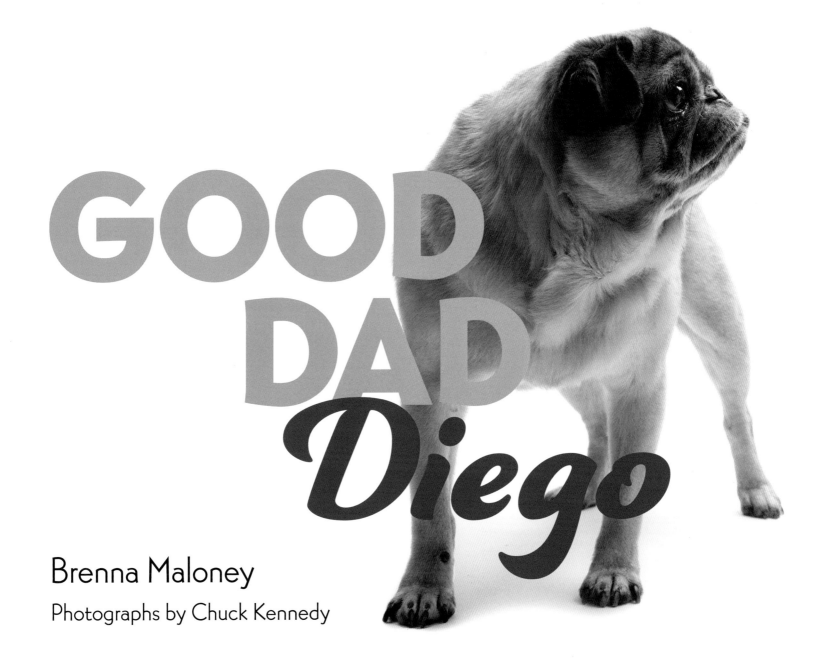

GOOD DAD Diego

Brenna Maloney

Photographs by Chuck Kennedy

Viking

This is Diego.

He has one of the toughest jobs in the world.

Is he a **superhero**?

Nope.

Is he a *ninja*?

No.

Diego is a
dad.

You might think that makes him *king* of his castle.

But as a dad, Diego has to be many things for his family.

He wears a lot of hats, not just a crown.

Sometimes, he has to be **"*The Law.*"**

"Stop digging up the plants!"

"No pooping on the floor!"

"Don't eat cat barf."

Once in a while, he's the **cook**.
That usually means meat casserole.
Again.

*"What do you mean you don't like it?
It's meat. It's casserole."*

He's the **nurse** who fixes scrapes and scratches.

"Where is the boo boo? I will kiss it."

And the one who fixes
everything *else*, too.
(Even if it falls into the toilet.)

*"You dropped the what
in the where?"*

Sometimes it just seems like there's too much to do . . .

"Sigh."

But Diego wants to be a ***good dad***.

A good dad dives in
when the dishes stack up.

"I'll have these clean in no time."

He tackles those
piles of laundry.

"I'm on it."

He's ready to mop up messes.
All day. Every day.

"Again?"

But that's not all.

Part of being a good dad is setting a good example, too.
Diego always wears his winter hat when it's cold outside.

"I look like an elf."

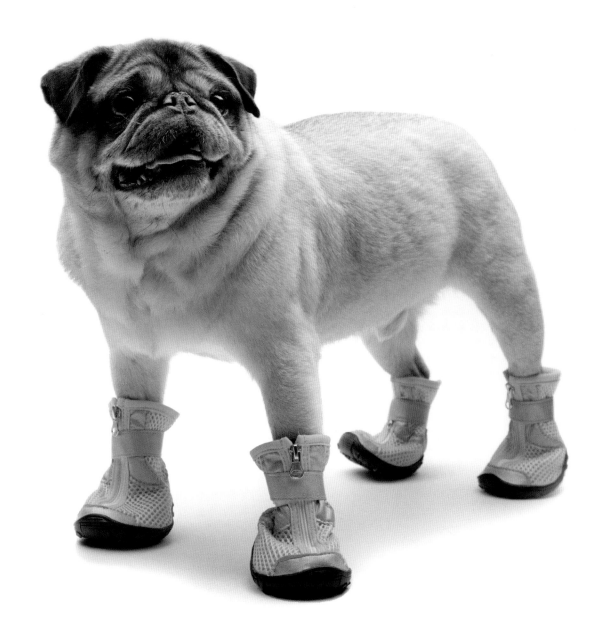

He always wears his booties
when it rains.

*"Rain or snow, I wear these
wherever I go!"*

Being a dad is hard work.
There's never any time just for Diego.

But, he doesn't really mind . . .

It's all part of being a . . .

"Daaaaaad!"

"Dad!"

"Daddy?"

"Dad."

"Dad, Dad, Dad, Dad,
Dad, Dad, Dad . . ."

Dad!

"That's me."

Dedicated to my dad,
who is, did, and does all these things.

And to Rollo—you will always be my little potato.

VIKING
Penguin Young Readers
An imprint of Penguin Random House LLC
375 Hudson Street
New York, New York 10014

First published in the United States of America by Viking, an imprint of Penguin Random House LLC, 2019

LIBRARY OF CONGRESS CATALOGING-IN-PUBLICATION DATA IS AVAILABLE
ISBN 9780451481269

Manufactured in China

1 2 3 4 5 6 7 8 9 10

The dignity of all pug dogs was carefully preserved during the making of this book, despite the wearing of silly hats.

Deleted Scenes